The Voyage

Written by Donald C. Mitchell
Illustrated by Susan Guevara

STECK-VAUGHN
COMPANY
ELEMENTARY · SECONDARY · ADULT · LIBRARY

Contents

Poncho and Grandpa

Poncho de Leon was a curious young hermit crab. He loved to sit on the beach and listen to his grandpa tell stories about the sea. Grandpa told him about the many islands he had found when he was an explorer.

"Do you wish you were still an explorer?" asked Poncho.

Grandpa told Poncho, "Not really, except I still wish I had discovered Lost Island. It has never been found. Stories say it has amazing waterfalls, strange birds, and even a volcano."

Grandpa gave Poncho a wrinkled old map. He said, "This map shows some of the islands I discovered. Do you think you could find Lost Island?"

Poncho said, "I'd like to try. I could sail through the Gulf of Pineapple and use your old map to guide me."

Poncho was very excited. He wanted to be a great explorer like Grandpa. Poncho set to work. First he made a list of all the things he'd need on his voyage.

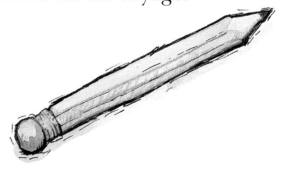

N
W E
S

Gulf
of
Pineapple

Lost Island
should be here

New
World

THINGS I NEED

- bedsheet (for a sail)
- broomstick (for a mast)
- driftwood (for a boat)
- Maps (Grandpa's map
     and a newer map)
- radio (for weather reports)
- food (crackers, dried fruit,
     gummy fish candy, water
- telescope
- flashlight
- rope
- wooden spoon
- compass

For the next week, Poncho got ready for his sea voyage. He showed his list to his grandfather. Grandpa read it and smiled. Then he said, "You'll need one more thing." He handed Poncho his captain's hat. "This is for good luck."

Poncho worked hard. He got some driftwood and made it into a boat. He used the broomstick for a mast, and he used a bed sheet for the sail. He added a small wooden box for a cozy cabin. It would be a good place to sleep and to stay when it rained.

THINGS I NEED
bedsheet
broomstick
driftwood
Maps
Radio
food
Telescope
Flashlight
Rope
wooden spoon

7

Setting Sail

Poncho sailed off to search for Lost Island. He used a wooden spoon to steer the boat out of the harbor and into the Gulf of Pineapple. The weather was warm with light winds. A gentle breeze moved the boat through the water.

Poncho sailed for most of the first day. He was tired, but he felt excited about his big adventure. "I am on my way to the islands," said Poncho to himself. Then he yelled, "I AM ON MY WAY TO LOST ISLAND!" He was all alone and no one could hear him.

The next day, Poncho saw a huge, sleek shape moving through the water. It leaped high into the air and then dove deep. It was a dolphin! The dolphin swam ahead of Poncho. After a while, it came closer. Poncho asked, "Are you hungry? Would you like some fruit?"

The dolphin laughed and then said, "Dolphins don't eat fruit. Thanks, but I have plenty to eat in the sea. Would you like some seaweed?"

"I've never had seaweed, but I'll try it," said Poncho.

Soon Poncho and the dolphin, named Marco, became good friends. Poncho was happy to have a friend to share his trip.

The Islands

The weather was perfect for sailing. After one week at sea, Poncho spotted an island. As Poncho and Marco got closer, Poncho saw that the island was covered with fruit trees. Each tree had

different kinds of fruit on it! He had
never seen that before.

Poncho steered the boat to shore and
loaded some fruit on board. He opened
a coconut with a large rock. He ate the
juice and fruit. Even Marco tried it.

The next island Poncho and Marco saw seemed to have a million seagulls on it. Seagulls nested on the beach, on the hills, and in the trees. When Poncho remembered that seagulls liked to eat hermit crabs, he paddled past the island.

Later that day, Poncho and Marco met a school of flying fish! Poncho had never seen fish that could fly, but Marco knew all about them. Poncho was amazed to see them fly over the sea. Marco swam and jumped with them awhile. Then they sailed on, hoping to discover Lost Island.

A Big Scare

Poncho wondered if they would ever find Lost Island. They used Grandpa's map to guide them. They also studied Poncho's new map.

Poncho was turning the boat when suddenly a huge octopus grabbed the little boat. It tossed the boat high above the water. Poncho was sure that he was doomed. Then Marco turned around and started swimming away. Poncho thought that Marco was leaving because he was afraid of the octopus. What would happen now?

Just when Poncho started to give up hope, Marco turned around and swam full speed ahead toward the octopus. Marco swam straight into the side of the octopus. He struck it so hard that it let go of the boat. Then the octopus swam away from the two good friends.

Poncho cried out, "Marco, you saved me!" Poncho and Marco jumped for joy. Poncho and Marco promised always to take care of each other. Poncho was sure they could make it to Lost Island now.

Lost Island

The next day, there was a new sight on the horizon. At first, it looked like a small bump. Soon Poncho and Marco saw land around the bump. When they sailed closer, they saw that the bump was really a mountain. It was an island with a mountain on it.

Poncho and Marco felt excited. They thought this might be Lost Island. The island was covered with beautiful green trees. Strange looking birds sang pretty songs. Smoke was coming out of the mountaintop. The mountain was a volcano. They had found Lost Island!

Poncho went on the island to explore. Soon he fell asleep under some trees. He woke up to loud rumbling and shaking. The ground was moving. Smoke was everywhere. Poncho ran to the boat. Marco pulled the boat away from the island.

As they raced away from Lost Island, red hot lava poured out of the volcano

and covered the whole island. Suddenly,
the island disappeared into the sea.

"Who will believe that I ever found
the island?" thought Poncho. Marco
pointed to a strange bird that was on top
of the mast. Poncho smiled. He knew
Grandpa would believe him if he brought
the bird home.

The Storm

Poncho and Marco knew it was time to go back home. As they sailed away from Lost Island, the sky turned gray and dark. A storm was coming, and they had to sail through it to get home.

The storm struck quickly and tore the sail off the mast. Next, the mast broke into pieces. The boat flipped around and around. Then the strange bird flew into Poncho's cabin. Poncho tied himself and the bird to a pole.

While the boat was being tossed all about, Marco just swam around the boat. He couldn't help Poncho this time.

24

Somehow the little boat held together until the storm ended. But it started leaking badly. "What can we do now?" asked Poncho.

Marco said, "Do you have any coconuts left in the boat?"

"Yes, but why think of food at a time like this?" asked Poncho.

Marco said, "Coconuts float. You can tie them together to make a raft. Then you can float home."

Marco helped Poncho tie the coconuts together. They built a raft just big enough for Poncho and the bird to get home.

Home at Last

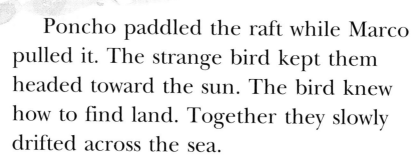

Poncho paddled the raft while Marco pulled it. The strange bird kept them headed toward the sun. The bird knew how to find land. Together they slowly drifted across the sea.

After many days, the strange bird spotted land. Marco swam ahead. Then he swam back with a huge smile on his face. Poncho's grandfather was waiting for them on the beach.

Poncho gave Grandpa the strange bird as a present. Then Poncho told his grandfather about their voyage.

Grandpa asked, "Did you find any of the islands we talked about?"

"I sure did, Grandpa. The best island of all was Lost Island," said Poncho. "The island was as beautiful as you described. There were waterfalls, beautiful trees, and strange birds. But Lost Island is really lost now. We saw red hot lava pour out of a volcano and cover the island. Then we got away just in time. The only thing left is this strange bird." Just then, the bird began to sing.